This Little Tiger book belongs to:

_____

_____

_____

To Ella
who is a beautiful
❋ 🦋 ❋
butterfly

LITTLE TIGER PRESS
1 The Coda Centre, 189 Munster Road,
London SW6 6AW
www.littletiger.co.uk

First published in Great Britain 2004
by Little Tiger Press, London
This edition published 2013

All rights reserved • ISBN 978-1-84895-776-3
Printed in China • LTP/1900/0678/0513
2 4 6 8 10 9 7 5 3 1

The Very Ugly Bug

Liz Pichon

Little Tiger Press

There once was an ugly bug.
A **very** ugly bug.

All the other bugs were a bit ugly,
but she was by far the ugliest.

She had **huge** googly eyes,

a lumpy, wibbly-wobbly head,

a horrible hairy back,

and spotted purple legs.

What a sight she was!

The very ugly bug wondered why the other bugs didn't look like her.

"Spotty red bug, why are your eyes so teeny tiny and not big and googly like mine?"

"My eyes are teeny tiny so I can hide in the berries and be safe from birds," said the spotty red bug.

"Skinny green bug, why is your back so smooth and green and not hairy like mine?" asked the very ugly bug.

"My smooth green back means I can hide in the leaves and be safe from birds," said the skinny green bug.

"Shiny blue bug, why do you have such big fluttery wings? I don't have any wings at all," said the very ugly bug.

"I use my big fluttery wings to fly away from birds, high up in the sky . . ."

"like this!" said the
shiny blue bug.

Whoooooooooooooooosshhh!

"Hmm," thought the very ugly bug.

Nothing here!

"If only I had teeny tiny eyes, a smooth green back and

So the very ugly bug decided that she would make a mask to help her eyes look teeny tiny.

She used a leaf
to make her back look
smooth and green.

She even found a
pair of fluttery
wings. "I'll be safe
from birds now!"
she said.

But she wasn't safe at all. The funny disguise made her stand out even more! Now everyone could see her—including a big hungry bird in the sky.

"Yum, yum," said the bird. "Look at that lovely juicy bug down there. It looks delicious!" And he flew down for a tasty bug snack.

I can still see her.

So can I . . .

Oh, dear.

"ARGH!" yelled the very ugly bug as the bird swooped closer. The other bugs quickly hid and flew away. Then suddenly, something very strange happened.

The big scare made the very ugly bug even uglier.

Her big googly eyes got bigger.

Her lumpy head began to wiggle and wobble.

Her horrible hairy back spiked up,

and her spotted purple legs waved in the air.

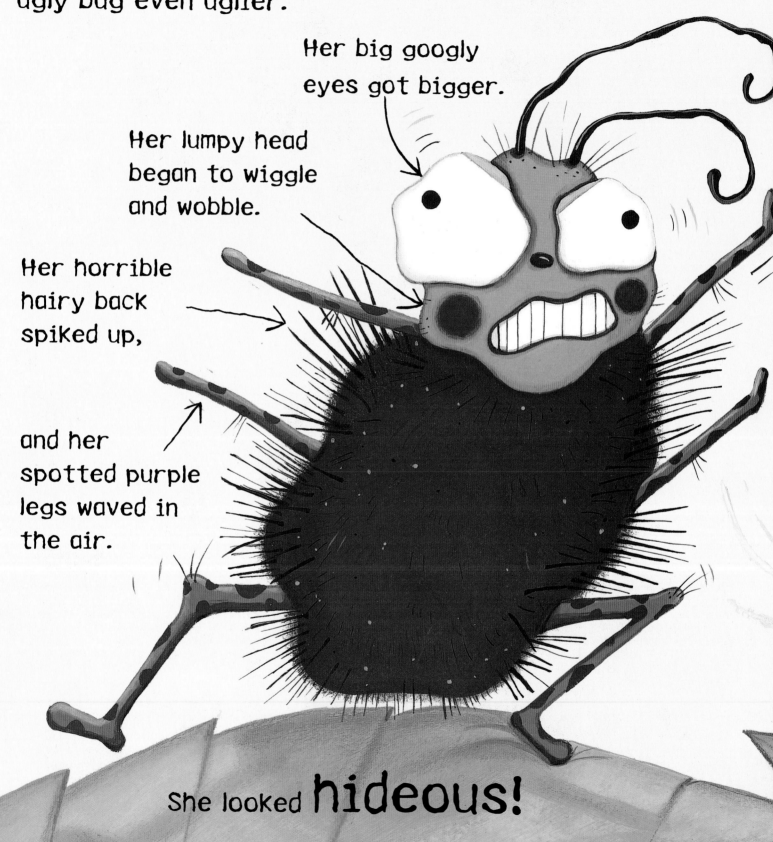

She looked hideous!

"Ugh!" said the bird. "That bug doesn't look tasty at all! It will give me a tummy ache." So he flew off to look for a nice, juicy caterpillar instead.

"Hooray for the

very ugly bug!"

cheered the other bugs. "She's so
ugly, she's scared the bird away!"

"Now I love the way I look!" said
the very ugly bug proudly. And Mr.
Ugly Bug agreed. He thought she
was gorgeous.

The two ugly bugs fell in love and had
a big family of baby bugs . . .

who were all even uglier than their parents!

Love Bugs